15.50

Before the Picnic

by Yoriko Tsutsui

illustrated by Akiko Hayashi

Philomel Books · New York

First American edition, 1987
Text copyright © 1980 by Yoriko Tsutsui. Illustrations copyright © 1980 by Akiko Hayashi.
American text copyright © 1987 by Philomel Books, a division of The Putnam Publishing Group,
51 Madison Avenue, New York, NY 10010. Originally published by Fukuinkan Shoten, Tokyo.
All rights reserved. Printed in Japan. Designed by Martha Rago. First Impression.

Sashi jumped out of bed and
opened her curtains.
It was a perfect day for the picnic.

She went downstairs for breakfast.
Mother was busy cooking food
for the picnic. Sashi knew how
she could help Mother get ready.

"See, I've packed our lunch,"
Sashi called to Mother.

Sashi went to see what
Father was doing. He was busy
shaving, but Sashi knew how
she could help Father get ready.

"See, I've packed our bags!"
Sashi called to Father.

Mother helped Sashi put on
her dress for the picnic.

Sashi knew how she could help
herself get ready too.
"I need to be pretty for the picnic,"
she said.

"We can go now," Sashi told Mother.

Mother cleaned Sashi's face
with a towel, and Sashi
went outside to wait.

Before she knew it,
she was all dirty,

and she had to get dressed all over again.

At last Mother and Father were
ready to go on the picnic.
Sashi was ready too.

She knew it would be a perfect day.